DIARY

OF A
MINECRAFT
ZOMBIE

Book 10

Zack Zombie

Saturday

"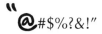#$%?&!"

"Wesley! What did you say?!!!"

"@#$%?&!"

"Wesley! Where did you learn that word?!!"

"Zumby tode it to me."

"ZOMBIE! GET IN HERE RIGHT NOW!"

Oh boy… I think I'm in real trouble now.

"Yes, mom?"

"Zombie! Did you teach your little brother that bad word?"

"What bad word?"

"I'm not going to repeat it."

"But then how am I going to know what word it is?"

I kind of figured I could outsmart my Mom and get out of whatever trouble I was in.

"Well, I'm going to spell it for you. The word is @ - # - $ - % - ? - &."

"Oh, you mean @#$%?&!"

"ZOMBIE! Don't use that word!"

"What's wrong with @#$%?&?"

"Zombie!"

I have to admit, I kind of liked the way that my mom turned a weird shade of green every time I said that word.

"What? The kids at school say @#$%?&! all the time."

"Zombie! Humph! Maybe your father can help you understand this better."

"FRANCIS!"

"Yes, honey? Did I do something wrong?"

"Your son thinks that saying the word, @ - # - $ - % - ? - &, is OK."

"Whoa! Zombie, when I was a kid, if I ever used that word, my mother would've washed my mouth out with slime."

"But Dad, what's wrong with @#$%?&? The kids at school say it all the time. I even heard the mail man say it one day when the neighbor's wolf bit him."

Something told me that I just found a secret weapon that I can use to make the adults in my life get all crazy.

"Zombie, just because the kids around you use it, doesn't mean you have to," my Dad said.

3

Meanwhile, Wesley was having fun practicing the new word he learned.

"@#$%?&!, @#$%?&!, @#$%?&!, @#$%?&!"

"Wesley! Don't use that word, it makes people very sad," Mom said, trying to appeal to his overwhelming sense of compassion.

"@#$%?&!, @#$%?&!, @#$%?&!, @#$%?&!"

"FRANCIS! DO SOMETHING!"

I started getting nervous when my Mom's color changed from green to a bright red. I actually didn't know that Zombies could do that.

"Zombie, you're going to have to fix this," my Dad said. "Wesley is as at an age where he's going to listen to his big brother more than his Mom and Dad."

"Really?"

Whoa! I have more power than my Mom and Dad? Wow. I wonder what other secrets adults are hiding from us kids.

"Go ahead and try it," my Dad said. "You'll see."

"@#$%?&!, @#$%?&!, @#$%?&!, @#$%?&!"

Well, here it goes.

"Wesley, don't use that word."

All of a sudden, Wesley got really quiet as he stared at me with his big black eye sockets. Then I could tell he was about to burst out crying.

"Don't worry, Wesley, we're bros, right?"

Sniffle, sniffle. *"Yayah, weer bros, Zumby."*

Then I gave him a big bros hug.

After my Mom went back to her normal color, I could tell she was about to let out the waterworks too.

"OH, I LOVE MY BOYS SO MUCH!"

Hey, I'm not a hugger, but I knew if I didn't hug my mom right then, I was going be in some serious trouble for teaching my little brother that colorful new word.

"Come here, Mom."

HUUUUGGGGG.

Whew! That was close.

Sunday

"Dad, was it really true that your mom made you wash out your mouth with slime, when you used bad words?"

"Sure did. She did it so many times that my tongue turned greener than it usually is."

Wow. Who would've thought my Dad was so cool.

"Where did you learn the bad words from anyway?" I asked.

"Well, there was a new mob kid that moved into my neighborhood. He was a real rebel. His name was Dirk Blazelton. Once he moved in, all the kids on our block were getting their mouths washed out with slime."

"Whoa."

"Yeah. Like my Dad always said, 'It only takes one bad apple to spoil the whole bunch.'"

"Oh, OK, Dad."

I didn't really understand what my Dad was talking about. I really don't like apples.

But I really can't understand what all the fuss is about.

I mean what's wrong with bad words anyway?

I bet Steve doesn't get in trouble for saying bad words. Humans probably use bad words all the time.

Man, humans have the good life.

"By the way, Zombie, did your mother tell you that we're having a foreign exchange student stay with us for a few weeks?" my Dad asked.

What?!! Aww, man, there goes my booger collection.

"Really Dad? I hope he's not going to sleep in my room."

"Well, now that you mention it…"

"UURRGGGHHHHHH!!!!!"

"Don't worry Zombie, I already spoke to Rajit, and he seems like a really nice kid."

"Rajit? What kind of name is that? Where's he from, Dad?"

"His name is Rajit Venkatanarasimharajuvar-ipeta," my Mom said as she walked in the room.

It sounded like my Mom farted.

"Rajit what?!!"

"Actually, he said that you can call him *Raj* for short," my Dad said. "He's from the Endian Biome."

I've never heard of the Endian Biome before.

"He's the son of a really famous ambassador from the Endian Biome," Mom said. "So you should be very proud that he's staying at our home."

Great. An ambassador's kid. So when he snacks on my booger collection, he's going to do it with his little pinky finger sticking out.

"Don't worry, Zombie. It'll be fun. Plus, if you stay in Wesley's room it'll give you a chance to really bond with your little brother."

"Yeah, OK, Dad."

Wow. I thought I was done with the drama.

But here we go again.

10

Monday

"The answer is, GROOWWLLLLLLLL... THIRTEEN!"

"Um. Thank you, Zombie, for your answer," Ms. Bones said as she gave me a strange look.

Actually all the kids in class were looking at me like I had three eyes. Even the three-eyed kid looked at me strange.

"What's wrong, Zombie?" Skelee whispered to me.

"GRROOWWLLL. I DON'T KNOW!" I tried to whisper. But I think everyone heard me.

"I know what's happening," Creepy whispered. "Your voice is changing. It happens when you go through puberty."

"Puberty? Aw Man, I thought I was done with that... GROWLLLLL!"

Man, just when I thought I was done with puberty and all the weird things that happen to my body, now I have to deal with... GROWLLLL! this.

Wow, even my thoughts sound different.

I don't know what it's like for everybody else, but puberty for a Zombie is not fun.

Besides having my brain shrink to the size of a pea...

Besides one of my legs growing bigger than the other...

Besides growing multi-colored mold all over my body...

And parts of my body smelling different than others...

12

Now, my voice sounds like I swallowed a cactus.

But the worst change of all is that I'm also growing a new tooth!

Except it's not green, yellow or brown like my other teeth.

I'm growing a big, straight, white tooth right in the middle of my face, where my favorite hole in my smile was.

And I thought I was going to keep my beautiful baby Zombie smile forever.

Mom said I have to go to the dentist to have it removed.

Except, I don't know how I feel about the dentist.

I heard they drill in your teeth and stuff, and then you die.

Puberty.

…So, wrong.

14

Tuesday

"**H**ey, did you hear about the new mob kid that just transferred to our school?" Skelee asked me at lunch.

"No. Who is it?"

"His name is Blaze Blazelton. He's a Blaze from the Nether. They said that he was really popular at his old school… Well, at least before it burned down."

"Whoa."

Wow. Blaze Blazelton. That is such a cool name. I wish I had a cool name like that.

My name is not cool at all. I mean, what kind of name is Zack? I feel like my Mom and Dad sneezed right before they signed my birth certificate, and that's what came out.

But I can only imagine what it'd be like to have a really cool name like… Blaze Zombie-ton. Yeah!

If I had a name like that, I would get instant respect.

Or a name like Zander… Or Ace.

Or even Cash! Yeah… Cash Zombie-ton.

Man, I would be a legend.

Just when I thought that, I heard some music.

"BOOM! BOOM! BOOM! ARE YOU READY FOR THIS??!! BOOM! BOOM! BOOM!"

I don't know where the music was coming from, but all of a sudden the cafeteria doors burst open and in walks a mob kid surrounded in a Blaze of Glory.

"That's him! That's Blaze!" Skelee said.

Next thing I know all of the mob girls were fainting and falling all over the floor.

Even Sally, my ghoulfriend, looked like she grew her eyeballs back.

Well, if you didn't know, Sally and I have been on a little break since she got back.

She said something about me being a trouble magnet, and her needing a little less drama in her life since her parents split up.

I was really sorry to hear that her parents split up.

But she said it wasn't that bad. She actually said it happened a lot.

She said the good thing was they had plenty of extra body parts around the house to put them back together.

But, Man, Blaze made a really great entrance.

All day at school, I couldn't help thinking what it would be like to be Blaze for a day.

Man, I would be so red hot, not even Zombie Pigmen could handle me.

Wow, that would be the life.

Wednesday

"**W**hat's that on your face?!!!!"

"Look everybody! Zombie's got a tooth growing out of his mouth!"

"EEEEEEWWWWW!!!!"

That's all I heard when I got to school today.

It seems that my new tooth started growing even more overnight, and now it's bigger, whiter and brighter than ever.

20

I looked like I belonged on a human rap video.

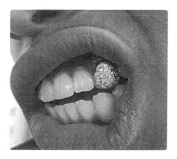

Man, I really miss my nice yellow, green and brown smile.

Worst part was that we had a field trip today, so on the bus that's all the other kids would talk about.

"Hey Zombie! Your teeth are so white, I bet when you close your mouth your eyes light up!"

"Hey Zombie! Your teeth are so white, I bet when you drink water it turns into milk!"

"Hey Zombie! Your teeth are so white, I bet when you walk into a church, everybody says, 'I see the light!'"

"Hey Zombie! Your teeth are so white, your mouth looks like piano keys!"

"Hey Zombie! Your tooth is so big, I bet when you sneeze you bite a hole in your chest!"

I'm just glad that we were going to the Minecraft Mob Zoo, so the trip was shorter than usual.

The Minecraft Mob Zoo was actually a lot of fun, so it took my mind off of my dumb tooth.

We got a chance to see wild wolves, ocelots, cows, pigs and I even saw a Mooshroom.

But what I really wanted to see was the wild Wither exhibit.

Now, most Withers are tame like my uncle.

But once in a while they capture one in the wild, and it is awesome!

They have to keep it in a cage made of unbreakable glass that is like 20 feet thick, so that it doesn't blast its way out of there.

Well, at least that's what Creepy told me.

"Whoa! Look at the size of that thing! It must be 100 feet tall!"

"I don't think it's that big, Creepy. Actually the sign says that it's only about 30 feet tall," I said.

"Man, it says that this Wither was caught in the Jungle Biome after it destroyed like 20 villages. They had to call in the Zombie Army to catch it," Slimey said.

"It doesn't look so tough now… I bet I can jump in there and ride it," somebody said behind us.

We all turned around and it was Blaze standing behind us with his mini crew of fans.

"That's because it's sleeping," Skelee said.

"Well, let's wake him up," Blaze said with an eerie smile.

All of a sudden, Blaze looked around to make sure no one was looking, and then he banged really loud on the glass.

Suddenly the Wither jumped up and hovered in its cage and gave me and the guys a really mean look.

Blaze started making funny faces at it and jumping around, making fun of it.

Then the Wither went crazy! It started to spin and fly around, and then it tried to blast its way out of the cage!

Suddenly an alarm went off in the Zoo, and everyone looked around to find out what was going on.

"ATTENTION! WE NEED EVERYONE TO EVACUATE THE BUILDING. WE HAVE AN EMERGENCY. THE ZOMBIE MILITARY HAS BEEN CALLED. WE NEED EVERYONE TO EVACUATE NOW!"

Everybody in the Zoo started to panic. Even the zookeepers looked worried, so I knew it was serious.

Ms. Bones got the whole class together and got us onto the bus quickly, and we drove away.

"What happened in there?!!" Ms. Bones asked all of us.

All the mob kids just looked at her, looking really scared.

"We should tell Ms. Bones what Blaze did," Creepy whispered to me.

"No way!" I said. "Then everybody will think we're tattle tales."

"Yeah, we're already pretty low on the popularity food chain," Slimey said.

So we all decided to stay quiet.

I glanced at the back of the bus and saw Blaze looking really proud, and all his groupies were looking at him like he was so brave.

To be honest, it was kinda cool how Blaze made the Wither get all crazy like that.

I wouldn't have had the guts to do that. Well, being a Zombie I actually don't have guts to do anything, really.

But man, that guy Blaze is really cool...

Thursday

Today I had to help out at the Principal's Office as part of the school's Student Volunteer program.

I had to show some new 7th grade foreign exchange student around school.

I thought that Rajit was the only foreign exchange student I had to deal with this semester. But it seems that there's a whole bunch of them visiting this year.

"Zombie, it seems that we're short on volunteers today," Principal Slime said. "Would you mind helping show one of the new 8th grade transfer students around school?"

"Sure, I can do that."

29

"Well, I'm pairing you up with a new mob boy that just transferred to our school. His name is Blaze Blazelton. Unfortunately his school burned down and this was the closest school to his town."

What! I'm going to have to show Blaze around school? Oh man, this is my chance to learn how to be cool.

"He's waiting for you outside of the guidance counselor's office. You can take next period to show him around the school."

"Sure thing, Principal Slime."

I started getting really nervous about showing Blaze around school.

What if he laughs at me? What if he thinks I'm a noob?

Oh, No! What if he notices…my new tooth?!!

I figured maybe I could hide my tooth
somehow before I met up with Blaze. So I ran
to the bathroom to do a quick makeover.

I was trying to find something to cover up my
tooth, but I couldn't find anything decent that
I could put in my mouth. I ran outside and
saw one of the classrooms open. I grabbed a
stapler from the teacher's desk and ran back
to the bathroom.

I figured if I kept half my mouth shut, Blaze
couldn't see my new tooth.

It took me a few tries to get the stapler
working right. I accidentally stapled my lip
to my eyelid so I looked like I was eating my

face. But after a few tries and a few pieces of rotten flesh later, I finally got it right.

I looked in the mirror.

I didn't look so bad. A lot of the kids talk out of the side of their mouths. Makes them look really gangsta.

Then I walked over to meet Blaze.

"Heyr Braze? Wazzarppenin?"

"What?"

"I zed, wazzarppening?"

Blaze just looked at me strange. He acted like he had never heard anybody talk gangsta before.

"Whatever. Look, I don't know about you, but I got things to do, and I don't want to waste my @#$%?& time walking around this school."

Whoa! Did he just curse?!!

"What's your name?" he asked me. Then he looked down at my name tag. "Zack, huh? PFFFFFFTT!"

"Brut, my frenz can caw me Zumbry," I said.

"Alright Zack. Hey, you ever cut class before? Me and a bunch of the other guys are going get some eats at our favorite spot. It's not too far from here. Why don't you join us? We can ditch class and go have some fun."

Man, I really wanted to go. But I had never cut class before.

"Das' aight! Uh… I got some ubber things to do," I said out of the side of my mouth.

"C'mon Zack, you know you want to…"

"Uhhhhh…"

To be honest, I really wanted to go hang out with Blaze and his friends.

"Uhhhhh…"

33

"Well, that's cool. But don't tell on us, OK?" Blaze said as he looked at me with his fiery eyes. It felt like he looked right through me. And he didn't even have to look through the hole in my head.

"Don't wully, I won't tell."

Then Blaze just gave me a nod and floated away.

Wow, even the way Blaze nods his head and floats away is cool!

Man, I really wanted to go with Blaze. I bet those guys are going to have so much fun.

And the way Blaze cursed made it sound so cool.

You know, I bet I could curse like that too.

I tried cursing under my breath so that no one could hear me.

But it sounded really wimpy and lame. Not like Blaze at all.

I need to say it with some real power, I thought.

So I ran to the bathroom and made sure no one was in there.

Well, here it goes…

"@#$%?&!" I yelled at the top of my voice.

There, I said it. And boy did I feel tough.

But, it still didn't sound as cool as when Blaze said it though.

So, I tried it like ten more times.

But for some reason I still couldn't get it right.

I guess I can try it again in a few days after my lips grow back.

Friday

CLINK!

CLINK!

"Don't worry, Zombie. There are a lot of zombies that don't have lips," the dentist said. "It makes them look kind of, you know, 'old school.'"

"Rrearry?"

CLINK!

"I think this is the last staple."

CLINK!

"There you go. Good as new. Now let's take a look at that tooth."

SHIIIINNNNE!

"WHOA! That's bright. I've never seen a tooth that white before. It almost looks human."

"RUAT?!!"

"Just kidding. That is, unless you've been hanging around a lot of humans. They say that you become like the people you hang around with, you know."

Is he kidding me? Am I becoming human?

Man, I don't like the dentist. Especially this guy.

You know, for a dentist, his breath smells really bad. It smells like a mix of bubble gum, roses and minty freshness all mixed together. BLECH!

I didn't really want to go to the dentist. But my parents really sweetened the deal.

They said that if I went to the dentist I could get my own cellphone.

And I'm going to get the best cellphone ever made and download ever cool app that I can.

All my friends are going to be so jealous.

Actually, all my friends have cellphones except me.

Even Creepy has a cellphone. But it's not a smartphone. It's just a regular phone that he can use to call places.

I guess it's a "dumb" phone! Ha ha!

It only has about 20 apps. But my cellphone is going to have like a million apps. It's going to be awesome!

"OK Zombie, I'm going to drill your tooth down so it won't be so noticeable. Then I can paint it a nice yellow or green color if you like. We can even add some brown to spice it up a little bit."

BLECH!

I guess if I don't die from his drill, I'll probably die from his breath.

Maybe I can hold my breath like...forever.

After the dentist, my Mom took me home while my Dad went to Scarget to get my new phone.

The dentist fixed my tooth, so now it looks really good.

I chose a nice green color with brown polka dots.

The dentist said that he was an artist before he became a dentist.

I didn't believe him at first, but now it totally makes sense.

I think all artists smell like roses.

BLECH!

I couldn't wait till Dad got home with my new phone.

When I get it I'm going to download all the cool games like Angry Bats, Zombies vs. Plants, and Clash of Creepers...

Even Minecraft. I heard that was like the best game ever.

Oh man, I can't wait!

"I'm home!"

I ran downstairs because I couldn't wait to start playing with my new cellphone.

"Here you go son! Your very first cellphone!"

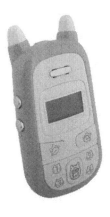

eeeeeehhhhhWAAAAAAAAAHHHHH!!!!!"

"What's the matter, Zombie?" Mom asked me.

"Yeah, buddy. Check out your new phone," Dad said. "It's got 4 buttons that you can use to call your Mom, or me, and you can even call your grandma!"

"WAAAAAAAAAAHHHHH!!!!!"

"Look Zombie, it even has 4 apps that you can play… See, it's got Bubble Dash, Chase the Ocelot, Butterfly Math, and Flower Power."

"WAAAAAAAAAAHHHHH!!!!!"

"I know they didn't have your favorite color, but the Zombie girl at the store said that pink is the new green."

"WAAAAAAAAAAHHHHH!!!!!"

"At least it goes with your lunch box," my Mom said.

"WAAAAAAAAAAHHHHH!!!!!"

Saturday

I cried myself to sleep yesterday, so before I knew it, it was Saturday.

"Do you feel better, Zombie?" my Mom asked as I came down for breakfast.

"Yeah… I guess so. Where's Dad?"

"Well, he felt bad about your cellphone, so he left early to get you one in your favorite color. He thinks they have a green one in another Scarget across town."

I didn't have the heart to tell Mom I hated that phone no matter what color it was.

"Great, Mom."

"By the way, don't forget that Rajit, the foreign exchange student, is coming today," my Mom said. "Your Dad is picking him on his way back from Scarget."

"He's coming already?"

"Yes, so please grab your things and take them to Wesley's room."

Oh man, I've got to spend a few weeks in my little brother's bedroom.

That's like the worst.

It wouldn't be so bad if Wesley wasn't always trying to get into everything that I do.

And when I'm playing video games he always wants to play. Then Mom and Dad make me help him the whole time.

And Mom and Dad always take his side.

UURRGGGHHH! Little brothers are such a pain.

But the one thing I am looking forward to is hiding in the closet and jumping out to scare him before bed.

I learned that from when Mom used to read me the book, *There's a Nightmare Human Kid in my Closet.*

That book creeped me out for months.

Now I get to shower the reign of terror on my little brother.

"MUUAAHAHAHAHA!"

"Oh, I think he's here," my Mom said.

I looked out the window and Dad was there along with this little square "thing" that was hopping next to him.

"Hey Mom, what's that thing next to Dad?"

"That's not a thing, that is a "HE" and his name is Rajit."

"That's Rajit? What is he?"

"He's a Shulker. They have many of them in the Endian Biome."

A Shulker? What in the world is a Shulker? I've hear of a shell and a lurker, but I've never heard of a Shulker.

"Hey everybody, we're home!" Dad said as he walked in. "I'd like you all to meet Rajit."

"Hello Rajit, it is great to meet you. This is my son Zack," Mom said.

"Hi, you can call me Zombie," I said.

"Hello, Zombie. My name is Rajit Venkatanarasimharajuvaripeta."

Man, every time I hear that name it sounds like someone farted.

"But you can call me Raj," he said.

"Zombie, why don't you show Raj to his room?" my Mom said.

I took Rajit upstairs, but all I was thinking about was my booger collection. I wanted to take it with me to Wesley's room, but it's gotten so dry and crusty that the jar stuck to the dresser in my room.

"Oh I see you have a booger collection!" Rajit said.

Aw man, there goes all those months of digging, hacking and picking down the drain.

"I have one back home," Rajit said as he took out a picture and showed it to me.

It looked like a picture of the Taj Mahal.

"So where's your booger collection?"

"That is my booger collection."

"Wha..?!!"

It was the Taj Mahal made totally out of boogers.

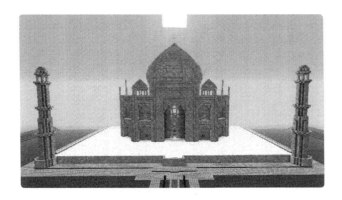

"Whoa. How did you collect so many?"

"Well, where I come from, it takes a village to raise a booger collection."

Wow, Rajit was crazy cool.

He said that his house was even bigger than his Taj Mahal booger collection.

"One day you must come visit my home. You can be my guest," Rajit said.

"Thanks, Raj."

Man, I can only imagine what it's like living in Rajit's house. He said his house is so big, that he has to take a limo just to go to the bathroom.

His house even has two zip codes.

I'm just wondering why he came to stay in our little shabby Zombie town.

I guess he wants to know how the other half lives.

Sunday

I went to go visit Steve today to see what he was up to.

I found him in his usual spot trying to punch a tree.

Except this time he was trying to use his new one-finger, tree destroying punch technique he learned from Mr. Matsumoto.

"Heeyaah!"

Dink.

BOOOMMM!!!

Well, I guess he doesn't have the hang of it yet.

"Wassup Steve?"

"What's cracking Zombie?" Steve said.

"Well, I got a pack of booger snacks in my pocket. Want some?"

"Oh… That's OK. Wassup buddy?"

"Hey Steve, can I ask you a question?"

"You just did."

"Can I ask you another one?"

"You just did."

"C'mon man, stop that."

"Alright. What's bothering you?"

"Hey, do villagers say bad words?"

"Some do. And some don't. But some villagers really curse a lot. It's like a second language."

"How come I've never heard you say bad words before?" I asked Steve.

"I used to. But then I decided I didn't need to anymore."

"Really? Why not?"

"Well, instead of cursing, I just go punch a tree."

"Seriously?"

"Yeah, cursing is just a way for people to get their anger out. For me, punching trees does the trick."

"You must get mad a lot. I always see you punching trees."

"Yeah... I guess so."

"But doesn't your hand hurt after a while?"

"You know, I've been punching trees so long, I never even noticed."

Wow. I used to think that saying bad words made people seem tough. But punching trees... You've got to be really tough to punch trees all day.

"Why're you asking?" Steve asked.

"Well, there's this new kid at school, and he's really cool. And he curses all the time."

"Let me guess... And you thought that if you could curse like him then you could be cool too?"

"Yeah."

"And then everybody would like you?"

"Yeah."

"And then you'd be the most popular kid in school?"

"Yeah."

"And then when you graduate, everybody will think you're a loser, because they're not impressed by your cursing?"

"Yeah… No… Wait, what?"

"Zombie, you don't need to curse to be cool. You can be cool just by being a really good friend to people. I bet you that Skelee, Slimey and Creepy think you're cool."

"Yeah."

"And I think you're really cool. And you don't curse around me or those guys."

"Wow. That's true."

"Zombie, anybody that needs to curse to be cool probably doesn't have any real friends."

Whoa. That's deep.

"Thanks Steve. I always feel so much better after talking to you."

"No problem, Z. But I'll see you later. I want to go back and finish practicing my new tree punching technique."

Man, Steve is so smart.

I wonder if I'm really becoming more human by hanging around him so much.

I really wouldn't want to be human, though.

They don't have enough boogers.

And I think I would get sick of punching trees all day.

BOOOOOMMM!!!!

Well, I guess Steve still has a little more practicing to do.

Anyway, what Steve said made a lot of sense.

But to be honest, it's kind of hard to believe.

I mean, Blaze always has a bunch of kids hanging around him all the time. And he's already the most popular kid in school.

How can he not have good friends?

Monday

"**Z**ombie! Can you please pick up your clean underwear?"

"Zombie! Can you please bring in the garbage?"

"Zombie! Can you please leave more rotten flesh all over the bathroom?"

"Zombie! Can you please start biting your toe-nails?"

"Zombie! Can you…"

"URRRRGGGHHHHH!!!! CAN'T YOU JUST LEAVE ME ALONE?!!!"

"Humph! How dare you talk back to me, young zombie!" My Mom said. "I'm going to tell your father when he gets home!"

58

URRRRGGGHHHHH!!!!

Why are my parents always picking on me?

I wish they would just leave me alone!

I can't wait till I'm old enough to move out of here. Then I won't have to hear…

Zombie, put away your sweet-smelling shoes, they reek.

Zombie, stop brushing your teeth or you won't get cavities.

Zombie, put on some indecent clothes, or you'll look like a human.

Zombie, if you don't pick your pimples they won't crater.

BLAH, BLAH, BLAH!

And then when I try to say something, I get in trouble.

I bet you Blaze doesn't get in trouble for talking back to his parents.

He's probably the boss in his house.

"Mom, do my chores," he probably says to his Mom.

"Right away, sir!" his Mom says.

"Dad, bite my toe-nails," he tells his Dad.

"With pleasure, Mr. President!" his Dad says.

"Sis, pick my nose," he says to his little sister.

"One or both nostrils, your eminence, sir?!" his sister says.

Then he probably just stays on his throne all day playing video games.

Man, I bet if I was more like Blaze, then my life would be so much easier.

60

Tuesday

Today was Rajit's first day of school.

I walked him to school so he could find his way.

"I'm not used to hopping around to get different places," Rajit said. "It is primitive, but very practical."

"How do you normally get to school?"

"Well, I just teleport to one of the rooms at our estate."

"You have a school at your house? Doesn't that mean that you're homeschooled?"

"Yes, I guess it does. Since it's the only school in our biome, then I guess everyone else is homeschooled at my house too."

Wow. It must be really nice being rich.

61

"Well, this is the principal's office. He'll probably assign you a buddy to show you around the school. I've got to get to class, so I'll see you later."

"Can you be my buddy?" Rajit asked me.

I felt bad for Rajit. Being a small runt in a new school is like being a baby chicken at a wolf convention. I thought about asking Principal Slime to move me, but I knew that if I became Rajit's buddy, I wouldn't be able to hang out with Blaze.

"I'm sorry, Raj, but those are the rules, and they're pretty strict. But I'm sure you'll find someone really nice who can show you around."

As I walked away, I looked back, and it looked like Rajit was rubbing his eyes or something.

Huh, must be allergies.

At lunch time, I was so happy because they were serving my favorite food... Cake!

I was so hungry that I grabbed a few pieces. The Zombie lunch lady saw how hungry I was so she gave me a few extra pieces more. Then I saw Skelee, Slimey and Creepy sitting down at our favorite table at the back of the cafeteria. So I grabbed a few more pieces for those guys too.

As I was walking over to sit with my friends, I passed the table with all of the cool kids. Suddenly, I noticed that Blaze was sitting in the middle, with all of the other kids just hanging around him.

Wow, Blaze has only been here a few days, and he's already the most popular kid in school.

All of a sudden, Blaze saw me.

"Hey Zack!"

Blaze yelled for me as the other kids looked at me like I had human cooties.

"He...hey... Blaze. What are you guys doing?"

"Hey Zack, why don't you talk like you did the other day... I told the guys you were a real gangsta."

So I tried talking out of the side of my mouth again. It was kind of hard without the staples, though.

"Sup, Braze. Wazzarppenin'?"

"PFFFFFTTT!!! HAHAHAHAHAHA!"

All the cool kids started laughing. And boy did I feel stupid.

"I told you he was cool. Hey, Zack, why don't you come sit with us?" Blaze asked me.

What? Blaze thinks I'm cool?

"Aight!" I said out of the side of my mouth.

"HAHAHAHAHAHA!"

I looked over at Skelee, Slimey and Creepy down at the back table, and they all looked real sad.

I guess they'll understand. It's not every day you get to sit at the cool kid's table.

"Hey, you don't want that, do you?" Blaze said as he grabbed a piece of cake off my tray.

Then all of the other kids grabbed some pieces, until I only had a few crumbs left.

Heh. It didn't matter.

I wasn't that hungry anyway.

Wednesday

Man, I can't believe that all the cool kids at school let me hang out with them yesterday.

And all because of Blaze.

Wow, that dude is so cool.

But yesterday I noticed that all of the cool kids were looking at my clothes and making funny faces and whispering to each other.

I felt kind of weird.

67

I also noticed that none of them were wearing a turquoise shirt and blue pants.

Oh man, is that it?!

Could the reason I've been unpopular my whole life is that I've worn the same clothes as long as I can remember?

Come to think of it, all of the unpopular Zombies wear the same turquoise shirt and blue pants.

I bet if I change my look I'll be as cool as Blaze, I thought.

But what should I change my look to? I mean, having the same shirt and pants makes life really easy for a Zombie in middle school.

Especially since I've never had to wash them.

But what's going to be my new look?

I got it!

Since Blaze is the coolest kid in school, if I just dress like him, then I'll be super cool too.

Hmmm. Let me see. Since Blaze is a Blaze, he doesn't wear any clothes at all.

Come to think of it, a lot of the other mob kids don't wear any clothes either, which is kinda weird.

But still, if that's what a brutha has to do to earn some respect, then I'll do it!

So goodbye turquoise shirt!

Goodbye blue pants!

Goodbye Squarebob Spongepants underwear!

Tomorrow, I'm going to be the coolest un-dressed kid in school.

Bring it!

Thursday

I got suspended from school today.

The principal said it was because of something called, "indecent exposure," whatever that means.

I mean I don't get it.

Half the school walks around naked, and they never get in trouble.

I mean, Endermen walk around naked...

Skeletons walk around naked...

Slimes walk around naked...

Even Creepers walk around naked...

But if a Zombie decides to go "AU-NATURAL," people just can't accept it.

72

Wow, so much for equal rights.

But I still need to come up with a cool new look…but one that won't get me suspended.

Hmmm…

I got it!

One thing about my Dad is that he doesn't throw anything away.

Since he used to be in a band when he was in high school, he used to collect all these cool music magazines. I bet I can get some good ideas from there.

It's kind of funny imagining my Dad in a band.

I think he said their name was the UNGRATEFUL DEAD.

73

It even had humans in it.

Yeah, my Dad was a real rebel in those days.

"Here it is!"

"Music of the 80's—Annual Edition."

I bet I can get a lot of great ideas from here.

Well, here goes nuthin'.

Thursday Late Entry

Well, I finally found my look.

Putting it together was a little tough, though.

It's a good thing that I found a bunch of Dad's old clothes in the trunk where he kept his old magazines.

For some reason there were a bunch of wigs in there too.

A little "TMI" that I didn't want to know about my Dad...

Anyway, I tried to take a "selfie" with my new cellphone, but it didn't have a camera.

I guess they didn't think a 13 year old zombie would need to take selfies.

Man, I hate this phone.

It's a good thing I found my Mom's camera in the trunk, though.

It was kind of old, but at least it printed the pictures out right away.

So here it is…Zombie 2.0!

So look out Mob middle school…

Zack is on the attack!

Friday

"Dude, what's that growing on your head?"

"You look like you grew a mustache but forgot where your nose was."

"You look like a sabre tooth tiger coughed up a hair ball and you caught it with your head."

"I didn't know that mold could grow all wild like that."

I guess the kids at school didn't appreciate my Dad's wig.

I got rid of it by second period.

I tried to flush it down the toilet. Except, I don't think it worked.

They had to evacuate the building because someone said they saw a giant rat floating out of the boy's bathroom.

I guess I'm going to have to do my new look without the "rug."

At lunch, all the cool kids were complimenting me on my new look.

There I was sitting with Blaze and the other cool kids, and nobody was making funny faces and whispering around me anymore.

Now they just made faces and talked about all the other kids.

"Hey, look at those three losers sitting at that table," one of the cool kids said.

"Yeah, those guys are really a bunch of @#$%?&!" another kid said.

"Hey, Zack, didn't you used to hang out with those losers?"

"Naw, not me. I don't know those guys," I said as I tried to avoid Skelee, Slimey and Creepy from seeing me.

"Hey, look at this weirdo walking in the cafeteria."

All the guys turned and started laughing at the little square kid that hopped into the lunchroom.

"HAHAHAHAHA!"

Oh man, what's Rajit doing here?

I tried to hide behind a Slime kid that was sitting next to Blaze so Rajit wouldn't see me. But, Rajit saw me and he waved at me.

"Look, the little noob is waving at us."

"HAHAHAHAHA!"

I started laughing too.

But next thing I know, Rajit lowered his hand, and then his shell closed around him and he teleported away.

"HAHAHAHAHA!"

"That's what he gets for messing with us, right Zack?" Blaze said as he patted me on the back.

"Yeah, right, Blaze," I said, as I laughed a little.

But the truth was, I felt terrible.

Then my shirt caught on fire.

Saturday

My Mom and Dad wanted to go visit my grandparents this weekend, and we brought Rajit with us.

Rajit was smiling and laughing, as if the thing at school never happened.

He even gave me a small booger sculpture that he made last night.

"What is it?" I asked him.

"It's an Elephant. We have many of those where I come from. It's the national mascot of the Endian biome."

"Thanks, Raj."

I felt really bad taking it, especially after the way I treated him at school.

But it was really nice. It looked like he used some Prime Grade A boogers to make it too.

It was shiny too. I could tell he spent a lot of time buffing it up real nice.

"We're here! Grandma and Grandpa's house!" Dad said.

Grandma and Grandpa Zombie are really cool.

They've been around a really long time.

I like coming to Grandma and Grandpa's house because they always give me and Wesley the coolest presents.

One year Grandpa gave me a set of Zombie Army replica soldiers from the last Zombie Apocalypse.

And Wesley got some Squarebob Spongepants action figures.

But Wesley would always start crying because my Zombie Soldiers would keep eating his Squarebob Spongepants action figures.

MUAHAHAHAHA!

Grandma and Grandpa have a cool house too.

It's got a lot of rooms and cool places to hide.

But the one place we can never go was in the attic.

One time when I was seven, I tried going up there. But Grandpa and Grandma found me and they got really mad.

But this time, I'm not going to get caught.

Yeah, I know. I probably shouldn't do it.

But I know Blaze wouldn't be afraid, and neither will I.

Grandpa keeps the attic key around his neck. So it's going to be a little tricky trying to get it.

But the good thing is that when Grandpa takes his afternoon nap, he's as dead as a doornail.

I'll just sneak it off of him and then I'll take a peek at what's really in the attic.

"Hey Zombie, what are you thinking about?" Rajit asked me.

"Oh, nothing." I said, trying to hide my evil plan.

"Really? Because you look really sweaty."

I knew that Rajit was going to follow me around the whole time we were at Grandma and Grandpa's house. So I had to let him in on the plan.

"Wow," he said once I told him. "That reminds me of the time we took uncle Vijay's shell off while he was sleeping. When he woke up, he was so surprised that he was naked, he teleported."

"Ha, that's funny, Raj."

"Well, no one has ever seen him since."

"OOOKAY then. No more practical jokes for you."

Later that day, Grandpa laid down on the couch for his afternoon nap.

ZZZZZZKKKKKKKKKZZZZZZKKKKKK!

"Wow, Grandpa sure is loud. He sounds like he's going through puberty. Ha ha!"

I don't think Rajit got it, because he just stood there staring at me.

"OOOKAY then! Let's just get this over with," I whispered.

So I tried to get the key from under Grandpa's turquoise shirt.

ZZZZZZKKKKKKKKKZZZZZZKKKKKK!

Oh man! Old Zombie people breath. Smells like roses and bubble gum, with a hint of mint. BLECH!

ZZZZZZKKKKKKKKKZZZZZZKKKKKK!

I finally got the key out from under Grandpa's shirt, but it got stuck in Grandpa's neck. He doesn't have much rotten flesh left there so it got stuck in his spine.

"@#$%?&!" I whispered under my breath.

"Zombie! You should not say such bad words. Your village would be so dishonored!" Rajit said.

Yeah, whatever. I thought.

Rajit wouldn't understand. I'm sure there aren't any cool kids where he's from.

Well, we spent about 20 minutes breathing in old Zombie people breath, BLECH! But we finally got the key from Grandpa.

"Hold on… Let me catch my breath… HUUUUHHHH! Alright, let's sneak up to the attic, and see what's in there."

"Zombie, I don't know if you should," Rajit said. "Where I am from, if people lock doors it is because they are trying to hide terrible things."

"They're my grandparents. What kind of terrible things could they be hiding in the attic?"

But then I thought about all the scary stories my Grandparents told us about all of the places they've been.

To be honest, I started to get a little scared.

"We should turn back Zombie," Rajit said.

I knew Blaze would never turn back. So I wasn't going to either.

"Naw, let's do this."

I stuck the key in the attic door keyhole. Then I grabbed onto the door knob.

Rajit couldn't look, so he just hid back in his shell.

Then I opened the door…

"AAAAAAAHHHHHH!!!!!!"

It was the most hideous, most terrifying sight I had ever seen!

My legs turned into spaghetti.

And whatever was left of my lunch, ended up by my feet.

Then everything got fuzzy and it all went black.

Sunday

All I could remember was waking up on the couch with my Mom, Dad, Grandpa and Grandma hovering over me.

"He's alive! Thank goodness," My Mom said.

"You had us worried there, son," My Dad said.

"Serves him right for peeking where he doesn't belong," Grandpa said.

"Oh Oswald, don't be so mean. Can't you see the boy almost died?" Grandma said.

As I looked around, I felt so woozy. But then I remembered!

"Rajit?!! Where is he?!! He was right behind me when I got attacked!!"

"Don't worry. If it wasn't for Rajit teleporting and finding us, you may not have made it," Dad said.

That's when I saw Rajit standing behind them.

Oh man, that was so close.

It was the most terrifying thing I had ever seen.

Why would my Grandpa and Grandpa keep those things in the attic?

Why would anyone keep things like that anywhere?

Old Zombie folks are so weird.

I will never look at them the same ever again...

For some reason Rajit wasn't scared at all.

91

"We have a whole room in my home filled with those," he said. "These are my favorites."

Then he handed me a picture.

Wha...?!!

"You should come to my house one day and I will show them to you," Rajit said.

I will never go to your house, ever, I thought as the rest of my lunch ended up by my feet again.

Monday

"Zombie, me and the guys are kind of worried about you," Skelee said.

"Yeah, Zombie. You've changed. You're dressing different, talking different, acting different...and you're even smelling different," Slimey whispered to me.

"Zombie, are you OK?" Creepy asked me.

Right then, Blaze and the crew walked in the cafeteria.

"Zack, you joinin' us?" Blaze asked.

"I'll see you clowns later!" I said really loud to the guys so that Blaze could hear me.

As I walked away and looked back, I saw the guys and they looked really embarrassed.

I kind of felt bad. But before I could think about it, Blaze started talking.

"Hey, let's cut class everybody. I'll meet you guys at our usual hangout," Blaze said.

"Sure thing, man," the guys said. "We'll see you later."

"Zack, you comin' this time?" Blaze asked me.

Man, I knew I shouldn't skip class. Especially because I had a test to study for.

But I couldn't miss this opportunity. It may never come again. I mean, opportunities like this don't happen often in the life of a middle school Zombie kid.

Gulp!

"Yeah. I'll be there," I squealed out.

"That's what I thought," Blaze said as he slapped me on the back.

Man, this is it. I've finally arrived.

Then my shirt caught fire again.

Tuesday

Wow, yesterday was so awesome.

I finally got a chance to hang out with Blaze and the cool kids and find out what they do when they cut class.

I kinda thought they were going to race their cars down some abandoned alley.

Or, I thought they were going out to scare villagers on the dangerous side of town.

Or maybe even get into a fight with some Silverfish gangs.

But they just sat around making fun of everybody at school.

Or they talked about how much they hated their parents.

"Parents are a real pain," one of the kids named Creeps said.

"Yeah, I can't stand my old man," another one of the kids named Slimo said.

"As soon as I graduate, I'm leaving and never coming back," a kid named Enderdude said.

"Yeah, parents are lame," Blaze said.

It wasn't exactly what I expected.

And I felt a little weird about how they talked about their parents.

But it was so cool anyway.

We stayed out all afternoon yesterday, so when I got home, I was too tired to study for my test.

So at school today, I was totally unprepared for our Mob Biology test.

97

The test was on Mob digestive systems.

I always wondered where the food goes after mobs eat.

Like, when a skeleton eats, where does the food go?

Or how about a slime? You can see right through them, and I never saw a stomach.

Creepy said that his stomach is in his feet.

I didn't really believe him until one day I tickled his foot, and he threw up.

I was really hoping that the test was about Zombie digestive systems.

I can just lift up my shirt and see where that food goes.

But when I got my test, I was doomed.

The test was about Endermen.

Man, I've never even seen an Endermen eat anything before.

In the middle of the test, I saw Jacob, the Enderman boy that sits a few rows in front of me, pull out a Scarburst candy out of his pocket.

Man, I lucked out! I thought. *Now I can see how an Enderman eats.*

Then Jacob took the Scarburst and put it under his arm…and it disappeared!

What…?

Then he took another one and did it again.

Man, it was gross, but it was exactly what I needed to answer most of the questions on the test.

Way to go Jacob!

Then Jacob did it again…and again…and again.

Nasty!

After the test was over, I came over to Jacob and asked him for a Scarburst.

"I don't like Scarbursts," he said.

"But I saw you eat like 30 of those things during the test."

"I wasn't eating Scarbursts. My armpits just get itchy when I get nervous."

Then Jacob pulled out an orange guitar pick and started scratching his armpits.

"Aaaahhh," he said as he scratched his armpits…vigorously.

Nasty.

Wednesday

"**H**ere you go, Zombie. And I cannot stress enough how disappointed I am," Ms. Bones said.

I couldn't even hear what Ms. Bones said, because all that I could pay attention to was the big fat red "F" on my test paper.

I looked over at Blaze. After he got his test paper, he was smiling and giving fiery fist pounds to the guys around him.

I don't get it. How did he pass and I didn't?

After class I asked Blaze how he did on his test.

"Read it and weep," he said.

There was a big fat green "A+" on his test paper.

"How did you pass the test? I mean, when did you get a chance to study?"

"Study? I don't need to study to pass a test," he said.

"Wha…?"

"Just hang out with me, Zack, and you'll never have to study for another test ever again," Blaze said.

Wow. That would be awesome. Imagine never having to study for a test for the rest of my life.

Blaze is my hero.

"Really? What do I need to do?" I asked Blaze.

"Well, our next test is on Friday. Just meet me and the guys tomorrow before school is closed."

"What are we going to do?"

"We're going to break into Ms. Bones' office and get a copy of test. Then we'll sneak out in the middle of the day so that we won't get caught."

"In the middle of the day?!!! That's crazy!!!! How are you going to keep from getting burned in the daylight?" I asked him.

"Don't worry about it, Zack. Once you hit puberty, mobs don't burn in the daylight anymore."

"Really?"

"Yeah. You're what…13. Yeah, you'll be fine."

Whoa, I never knew that, I thought.

Wow. Blaze is so smart.

"So this is what we'll do," Blaze said. "Tomorrow, before the end of school we're all going to hide in the janitor's closet. When the school closes we'll all go to Ms. Bones' office and take a pic of the test. When it turns daylight we'll all sneak out, and that's it. We're home free."

I got to admit, it sounded like a good plan.

But I felt bad because I said I wouldn't ever cheat on any tests ever again.

But the way Blaze explained it made it sound so cool.

Plus, I didn't want to let the guys down.

Wow, I never knew that Zombies didn't burn in daylight after a certain age.

No one ever told me.

Hmmm, I wonder what other secrets parents are hiding from us.

Thursday

Well, we did it.

We got the test just like Blaze said.

Now we're just waiting here till it turns daylight so that nobody will see us sneak out of the school.

I thought I would write in my journal to pass the time.

I still feel a little bad about cheating on the test.

But it feels so good to be wild and free.

And I couldn't have done it without my best bud Blaze.

That guy is so cool. If it wasn't for him, I'd still be a loser.

It really is true what they say, "You turn out exactly like the people you hang out with."

And I hate to say it, but I would still be a loser if I kept hanging out with the other guys.

"Alright guys, it's daytime" Blaze said. "Creeps and Slimo, you guys go first. Enderdude, you go with me. Zack, you got the most important job. You come out last to make sure no one is following us, OK?"

"Uh... Sure thing, Blaze," I said.

Then Creeps and Slimo went out into the daylight. I was really nervous until I saw that they didn't burn.

"See, I told you," Blaze said.

Then Blaze and Enderdude went outside into the daylight too. And they didn't burn either.

Blaze was right! Man, that dude is my hero.

I waited a few minutes to make sure no one was following.

Then it was my turn to go out.

Wow, this was so exciting. My first heist. So cool.

Look out world, here I come!

Friday

It's a good thing some sheep were around taking pictures yesterday.

They really helped me out of a jam.

Well, the good thing is I didn't have to take my test today.

110

I'm just thinking about what Blaze said about how after puberty mobs don't burn in daylight.

…Something tells me I'm a late bloomer.

Saturday

Today I was at home growing my skin back, when I got a surprise visitor.

"Steve! What are you doing here?"

"I came by to see how you were doing. You're looking a little crispy today."

"Yeah, I had an accident at school."

"Your parents told me," Steve said. "You know, I like your parents. They're really nice. Though I still don't understand why they're always holding their noses when they're around me."

"They're not used to human people smell. My Mom still thinks that humans smell funny."

"Yeah, I think your Dad forgot he was holding his nose when he shook my hand. I'll just leave it right here on your dresser if that's OK with you."

"Thanks for coming by," I told Steve.

"Yeah, the fellas told me you were going through some...well...you know...changes."

"Yeah, puberty is a real @#$%?&!"

"Whoa! Zombie, I thought you said you weren't going to curse anymore."

"Oh sorry, it just slipped out."

"You know Zombie, the guys are really worried that the new crowd you're running with are changing you," Steve said.

"Naw, they're pretty cool. Especially this new kid named Blaze. He's really cool. He's just like you...well, sort of."

"Really? Oh Ok. Well, then I bet he's a really good guy you can talk to and share all your problems with."

"Uh…no."

"But I bet he helps you to do better in school, right?"

"Uh…no."

"But I bet he really helps you figure out your parents so that you can get along with them better, right?"

"Uh…no."

"Well, at least he's straight with you and doesn't tell you to do anything that will hurt you, right?"

"Uh…"

"And, he's really cool with the people you care about like Skelee, Slimey and Creepy, right?"

"Umm…"

"And most of all, I bet he'll be your friend no matter how cool you are, no matter how you dress, and no matter how you look, right?"

"Uh… I don't know."

Steve just looked at me with that look that said, '*Zombie, you must be crazy…Snap out of it!*'

But all he said was, "Oh, OK… I'm sure he does other things that are really cool. He sounds like a really good friend."

"Uh… Yeah…thanks, Steve."

"Well, I gotta get going. But before I go, I got a surprise for you."

All of a sudden, Rajit walked in carrying a really big cake!

"Me, Rajit and the guys made it for you, with the help of your Mom of course. We thought you would want something to snack on while you grew your skin back."

"Wow. Thanks Steve..."

I didn't really want to say anything because I felt really choked up. I also didn't want to mention that the cake was a little creepy because it looked like Creepy.

"No worries, Zombie. We love you bro," Steve said. "See ya later."

Man, I knew I should be happy, but I felt really bad because of how I treated Rajit and the guys.

Wow.

I feel so confused.

Sunday

"ZOMBIE, WHAT DID YOU DO TO MY BABY?!!"

"What are you talking about, Mom?" I said, thinking that my Mom had gone crazy.

"Something is wrong with your little brother. All of a sudden he's talking back, he's saying bad words, and he even hit his pet chicken the other day."

"Well, what makes you think it was me? Maybe he saw something on TV or something."

"Oh, you really think you had nothing to do with it?" my Mom asked. "Well, then, take a look."

I went over to where my little brother was playing with his action figures.

"Wha...?"

And it got worse the more I heard Wesley talking and playing with his Squarebob Spongepants action figures.

"Hey, why don't you want to play wit me, Squarebob?"

"Cause I found sum better fwends than you, Patwick."

"But I lub you Squarebob, you're my best fwend."

119

"You're a clown. I'll see you lader, I'm going to go hang out wit my new fwend Bwaze."

"Squarebob, pwease don't leave me."

"Take that Patwick! Smash! Pow! Cwunch! Boom!"

"MUAHAHAHAHA!"

I went back to my Mom with my mouth hanging open.

"What do you have to say for yourself, young Zombie?"

"UHHHHHHH…."

"Don't Uhhhh me. I want you to go talk to your father this instant!"

I found my Dad in the living room watching his favorite show, Minecraft's Funniest Home Videos.

"Dad, Mom wanted me to come talk to you about Wesley."

"Whose Wesley? Oh, you mean the little juvenile delinquent that's playing in the next room?"

Gulp.

"Zombie, I told you that you're going to be the biggest influence in your little brother's life. Whatever you do, he's going to do it ten times more."

"But why me? I don't want to be a role model for anybody. That's just too much pressure for a 13 year old Zombie to handle."

"I know that's a lot of responsibility to handle. And I know you never asked for it... You probably never even wanted a little brother."

I didn't say anything about the last thing that Dad said. But it was true. I really never wanted a little brother. And now I can't have any fun in my life or my little brother will end up in Minecraft prison or something.

It's just so unfair.

"And I know you probably feel that it's really unfair," my Dad said.

"Mmhmm."

"And you probably think that you can't have any fun or your little brother will end up in Minecraft prison or something."

Whoa. How did he know that?

"But you know, having a little brother is like looking into a mirror. Whenever you look at him, he will always show you what you're really like inside."

"You mean like when Wesley was born, he looked like my appendix?"

"Uh… No. Just remember that your little brother will reflect all of the good or all of the bad that is in you."

I still didn't really get what Dad was talking about. I think it's because I don't have a driver's license.

"Oh, OK. Thanks Dad."

"I believe in you, Zombie," Dad said, and then he went back to watching his favorite show.

Man! Now I have to be careful about everything I do around my little brother.

He's going to get me in a lot of trouble with my parents if he keeps doing what I do.

But how am I supposed to get my little brother to stop doing bad things and start doing the kind of good things that won't get me in trouble?

Monday

Rajit asked me if I would walk with him to school today.

I kind of wanted to, but I didn't want to be seen around school with him.

Don't get me wrong, Rajit is a nice kid. But the other cool kids think he's kind of a loser.

"Sorry, Rajit, I've got to go to school early… Uh… I've got to catch up on some homework," I said.

"I need to catch up on some homework too," Rajit said. "I can join you."

"No, no…that's OK… Uh… I have some friends that I promised I would help them with their homework too."

"Don't worry, Rajit," my Mom said. "Zombie's father and I can drive you to school this morning."

"Thank you, Mrs. Zombie," Rajit said. "I very much appreciate your hospitality."

Then Rajit went upstairs to finish getting ready.

My Mom gave me a look like she was a little mad at what I said.

"Zombie, you need to be more hospitable to Rajit," she said. "Can't you see he needs your help?"

"What did I do now?!!"

"Don't talk to me in that tone of voice, young Zombie!"

"Forget this! I'm outta here!" I said as I slammed the door behind me.

"Zombie! Get back here right now!" Was all I heard in the background as I walked away.

I just thought about what Blaze would do.

So, I didn't even turn around.

I just kept on walking.

I don't get it, I thought. *First I mess up because my little brother. Now I mess up because of Rajit.*

Man, I can't do anything right in this family!

Maybe Blaze and the guys were right. Maybe parents are just a pain, and I need to get as far away from them as possible.

I was so mad that after my first period class I cut class and hung out with Blaze and the guys for the rest of the day.

School…

Who needs it anyway?

Tuesday

"**S**o, where is your homework, Zombie?"
Ms. Bones asked me.

I had a split second to decide what I was
going to say.

I could tell her the truth, and tell her I didn't
do it because I was goofing around with
Blaze and the guys all day yesterday.

But then I would get in trouble.

I didn't want to lie, because I remember all
the trouble it got me in last time.

"A wolf ate it," Blaze blurted out.

"Yeah, Ms. Bones. I saw it too," Enderdude
said.

"His eyes were all bright red and he was growling," Slimo said.

"Scared me to death," Creeps said.

Then Ms. Bones looked at me, and asked me, "Is this true, Zombie?"

"Uh huh," was all that squeaked out of my mouth.

"Then make sure you make up the homework tomorrow," Ms. Bones said. "And try to stay away from those wolves, next time. They can be dangerous."

Wow, the guys came to my rescue. None of my other friends would ever do that.

I looked over at Skelee, Creepy and Slimey and they just looked down like they were ashamed of what I did.

Then I looked over at Blaze and the guys, and they all gave me a thumbs up.

Hmmf! I don't need Skelee, Slimey and Creepy, I thought.

I've got some real friends now.

Wednesday

In the cafeteria today I overheard Blaze and the guys talking about something as I walked over to our table to eat my lunch.

"Man, that's going to be so boss!" Creeps said.

"Blaze, if you do it you are the man!" Slimo said.

"Yeah, Blaze. If you do that you're going to be a legend, bro," Enderdude said.

"You guys are doing it too," Blaze said. "Unless you guys are all chicken?"

"No way, count us in!"

It sounded like they were going to do something really cool… And I wanted to find out what, so I could get in on the action.

"What are you guys talking about?" I asked them.

"Blaze is crazy!" Creeps said.

"Yeah, but crazy cool!" Slimo said.

"What's going on, Blaze?" I asked.

"Well, you remember that day we went to the zoo?" Blaze asked me.

"Yeah."

"And you remember the big 30 foot Wither that was behind the unbreakable glass cage?"

"Yeah."

"And you remember I told you that I was going to ride it one day?"

"Yeah."

"Well, Friday, we're doing it! Me and the guys are going to sneak in after the zoo is closed and ride the Wither!"

"Whoa."

"And you're coming too."

"What?"

"Unless you're chicken. You're not chicken, are you Zack?"

Blaze and all of the guys were staring at me to see what I was going to say. It felt like they could see right through me, and not because of the holes in my head.

But I knew that if I chickened out, then I would go back to being the loser that I was, hanging out with my loser friends.

"I'm in!" I said, before I could talk myself out of it.

"Yeah! Zack, you're cool, man!" all the guys said.

"See I told you he wouldn't chicken out," Blaze said. "So hand over the money."

All the guys pulled out money and gave it to Blaze.

"What's the money for?" I asked them.

"Well, all the guys bet that you were a real loser and would chicken out," Blaze said. "But I knew you would do it cause you're a real gangsta."

Wow, I knew it! Blaze is my friend. He really does believe in me.

Man, it sure is good having a friend like Blaze who looks out for me like that.

Wow. I'm so lucky.

Thursday

Oh man, I'm really scared about riding the Wither.

You would think that I wouldn't be scared since my uncle is a Wither.

But my uncle is more like 1/3 Wither. He has sheep and rabbit in his blood so he's actually kind of small and harmless.

He still has three heads though, so he's really great at parties.

I started looking up some stuff online about the Wither that was at the Zoo.

I found an interview with the Zoologist that was part of the team that captured the Wither.

Reporter: Doctor please tell us a little about the Wither at the Minecraft Mob Zoo.

Zoologist: The Wither at the Minecraft Mob Zoo is a rare breed of Wither that has not been seen since prehistoric times.

Reporter: But where did it come from?

Zoologist: We believe this Wither is from the Zurrasic period when giant mobs roamed the Minecraft Overworld.

Reporter: Doctor, this is a big specimen. Do you expect it to get bigger?

Zoologist: We believe that this Wither is only a baby, but we expect it to grow to over 100 feet in size in its lifetime.

Reporter: So since it's a baby, it's safe then?

Zoologist: Don't get me wrong, just because it's a baby doesn't mean it's not dangerous. This Wither's blast is exceptionally dangerous and has the ability to destroy large areas, including villages.

In fact, this Wither destroyed 20 villages before we were able to subdue it, but only after the Zombie Military was called in to assist.

Reporter: How are you able to keep it so calm at the Zoo?

Zoologist: Most of the time we keep it lightly sedated through the use of soothing music in its cage. As long as nothing disturbs it from the very peaceful habitat we've created for it, it is relatively safe.

But if it were to be agitated, it could very well break through its cage and destroy the entire town.

"What are you reading, Zombie?" Rajit said as he walked in on me.

"Nothing!" I said as I closed my laptop.

"Were you looking at information about Withers?" Rajit asked. "Wild Withers are common where I am from. They are known to bring much destruction."

I really didn't want to hear that.

"I had an uncle that tried to ride a Wither once," Rajit said. "He thought that if he could ride a Wither, he would become the greatest mob in my village."

"What happened to him?" I asked.

"Well, I don't think he thought it through," he said with a sad look on his face. "You see, Shulkers don't have hands so…"

"Well, me and the guys are going to ride one tomorrow. And we're going to become legends!"

"Where are you going to ride a Wither?" Rajit asked.

"They have one at the Zoo. We're going to sneak in after it closes."

"Please don't do it, Zombie. It is much too dangerous!"

"Well, the guys I roll with eat danger for breakfast," I said.

"I cannot let you do this, Zombie!" Rajit said. "I must tell your mother and father."

"If you tell, my friends and I are going to mess you up. And that shell of yours is not going to protect you from us either."

As I walked away, I looked back and saw that Rajit had hid in his shell.

What a chicken, I thought.

As for me, tomorrow I'm gonna be a legend!

Friday

Me and the guys put bubble gum in the back door lock at the Zoo, so that we can get in after all of the Zoo keepers and security guards left.

"Is it open?" Blaze asked me.

"Yup. Easy money," I said.

As we all walked into the Zoo, we went over to the Wither exhibit. We got to the Wither cage and there it was sleeping in its glass cage.

I looked over at Creeps, Slimo and Enderdude, and they all looked really scared.

"Are we really going to ride the Wither?" Slimo asked. "I read on the zombienet that they're really dangerous."

"Yeah, I heard that this one destroyed like 20 villages before they captured it," Creeps said.

"Oh man, I think I'm going to be sick," Enderdude said.

"You guys aren't going to chicken out on me, are you?" Blaze asked.

But the guys just stayed quiet and looked at the ground.

"I'm ready!" I told Blaze.

"That's my man!" Blaze said. "Zack, I knew I could count on you."

All the other guys looked really ashamed as they looked at each other. Then, suddenly, they all ran away.

"Where are you guys going?!!" Blaze yelled after them.

Then Blaze started yelling curse words and going off in a rant.

143

"Those guys are just like those chickens that left me at my old school. I had to burn down the school all by myself."

Wha..? Did he just say what I think he said?

Then Blaze found the wall switch and turned on the lights.

The Wither was still sleeping…that is until Blaze turned off the soft music.

All of a sudden…

HUGGHHHRROOWWWWLLLL!!!!

Suddenly the Wither started shaking and making loud noises.

"C'MON YOU DUMB MOB!!!!" Blaze yelled at the cage.

And the more Blaze taunted the Wither, the more agitated it got.

"Hey Blaze! Uh… You sure you should be doing that?" I asked him.

"WHAT'S THE MATTER, LOSER?!!! YOU CHICKEN?!!! YOU GONNA RUN AWAY TOO?!!!

Whoa. Something's gotten into Blaze.

"Uh… Blaze… You sure you thought this through?" I asked him. "I mean, you don't have any hands and…"

"SHUT UP, YOU @#$%?&!" Blaze said. "I KNOW WHAT I'M DOIN'!"

Wow, something was definitely wrong with Blaze. It was like he had a death wish or something.

Blaze just kept taunting the Wither until finally…

BOOOMMMM!!! BOOOMMMM!!! BOOOMMMM!!!

The Wither shot multiple blasts at the cage.

"HAHAHAHA! YOU CAN'T TOUCH ME! HAHAHAHA!"

BOOOMMMM!!! BOOOMMMM!!! BOOOMMMM!!!

"HAHAHAHA!"

BOOOMMMM!!! BOOOMMMM!!! BOOOMMMM!!!

"HAHAHAHA!"

BOOOMMMM!!! BOOOMMMM!!!... *CRIK.*

Oh boy.

KAAABOOOOOOOOMMMM!

All of a sudden, the Wither blew the glass cage apart.

He was out!

I ducked under one of the tables as I heard the Wither chasing Blaze around.

HUGGHHHRROOWWWWLLLL!!!!

"MOMMY! MOMMY! MOMMY! MOMMY!" was all I heard.

BOOOMMMM!!! BOOOMMMM!!!

"AAAAHHHHHHHHH!!!!"

BOOOMMMM!!!

Then silence.

Oh man. The Wither killed Blaze!

But then I realized… I was next!

HUGGHHHRROOWWWWLLLL!!!!

BOOOMMMM!!!

Suddenly the table that I was hiding under was blown away.

And then I looked up, and there it was, the giant 30 foot Wither hovering over me.

HUGGHHHRROOWWWWLLLL!!!!

This was it. This was the end.

In that split second my 13 year old life flashed in front of my eyes.

I remembered when I first met Skelee, Slimey and Creepy when we were kids.

I remembered the day Steve saved me from being stepped on by an Iron Golem.

I remembered when Mutant saved me from getting my head knocked off by a Dodgeball.

I remembered when a gang of misfit mobs from Cabin Zero won the Moblympics at Creepaway Camp.

I remembered when my cousin piggy, Steve and my little brother Wesley helped me find my way to my 100th Zombie Family reunion.

And I remembered fighting the Zombie Apocalypse side by side with the best friends any Zombie could ever have.

Wow, for a Zombie with a pea brain, I sure do remember a lot.

But then everything became crystal clear.

Steve and the guys would never have put me in danger like this.

Steve and the guys wouldn't care how cool I was, or what clothes I wore, or what I looked like.

Steve and the guys would never leave me alone when I needed them the most.

And they would be my friends no matter how much of a loser I thought I was.

Man, I wish they were here… Sniff… Because then I could tell them how sorry I was, and how much they really mean to me.

HUGGHHHRROOWWWWLLLL!!!!

Then the Wither hurled a giant Wither skull blast at me.

This was it.

As the Wither skull came closer, I knew it was the end.

So I closed my eyes, and surrendered to my fate.

BOOOMMMM!!!

Wait a minute?

As I opened my eyes, I realized that I was floating!

The Wither kept hurling Wither skulls at me but I was floating away and dodging each blast.

Then I saw the Wither turn its head and roar.

I looked over, and saw Rajit, Steve, Skelee, Slimey, Creepy, and my Mom and Dad all throwing things, and yelling at the Wither.

Suddenly I floated over to where they were.

"How did you guys do that?" I asked, amazed.

"It wasn't us, it was Rajit!"

"Rajit, how did you do that?"

"We Shulkers can do a lot of interesting things," Rajit said. "We are a lot cooler than we look."

Suddenly the Wither started blasting us with Wither skulls.

"EVERYBODY MOVE!" Steve yelled.

We all dove out of the way as the Wither kept sending blast after blast after us.

We ran into the closet as the Wither spent the rest of the time destroying the Wither exhibit room.

"We need to put him back to sleep," I said. "We need to get over to the control panel and turn on the music."

"That's on the other side of the room," Skelee said. "The Wither will pick us off one by one before we even get close."

"Someone needs to distract him," Steve said. "I'll go."

"Steve, you can't," I said. "The Wither's too powerful. You can't punch your way out of this one."

All of us were just staring at each other. We all knew that whoever was going to be the distraction would probably never be coming back.

"Hey, where's Rajit?" Dad asked.

We all turned around, and the closet door was slightly open.

"Oh no…"

We ran out and there was the Wither, sending blast after blast at Rajit's shell.

"His shell can't take damage for any longer," Dad said. "If we're going to go, we need to go now."

"Let's do this," Steve said.

Skelee pulled out an arrow and got his bow ready.

Steve had a sword and a pickaxe in each hand.

Slimey blew himself up to twice his normal size. He also covered himself in Slime blocks to deflect any blast.

Mom, Dad and I hid behind Slimey, so we could make a dash for the control panel.

And Creepy just hissed... So we left him in the closet.

"Let's go!"

We all ran out as Steve and Skelee ran toward Rajit's side to distract the Wither.

Slimey made a great shield for Mom, Dad and me, and we slowly made our way closer and closer to the control panel.

But somehow…the Wither saw us.

He shot a giant Wither skull at us that would've stopped us in our tracks.

Slimey tried to protect us, but he was blasted out of the way and hit the ceiling like wet toilet paper.

Then the Wither sent another skull blast at Mom, Dad and me.

But suddenly, Rajit peeked out of his shell and shot what looked like giant spit balls at us.

Then right before the Wither blast hit us, we all started floating!

Steve and Skelee took the opportunity to make a final attack on the Wither and distract him again.

It was just the time we needed for Rajit to float us to the control panel safely.

"Quick, turn on the music!" I said.

Dad hit the controls for the music right when the Wither was about to blow Steve and Skelee to smithereens.

Suddenly, the Wither stopped in his tracks.

"It's working!" I said as the Wither started slowing down.

Rajit shot some more giant spit balls at the Wither, and got control of him. He then started rocking the Wither back and forth like a baby.

Slimey put out some Slime blocks on the ground, and Rajit put the drowsy Wither down on the Slime block bed.

Next thing you know, it was fast asleep.

"Aww, he looks so cute," my Mom said.

"Really Mom?" I asked.

"Whew! That was close," Skelee said.

"Yeah, if all you guys weren't here, I'd be a gonner…like Blaze," I said.

We all just stared at each other for a minute knowing what that meant.

"Hey, you guys hear that?" Dad asked.

We all heard what sounded like sniffles.

Everyone looked around to find out where it was coming from.

"It's coming from that box," Steve said as he went over to what looked like an old apple cart.

When he lifted the lid, suddenly we all heard, "Mommy! Mommy! Sniff. Sniff."

"Oh, so this must be your friend Blaze," Steve said as he and all the other guys held back their laughter.

"Hey, aren't you Dirk Blazelton's kid?" my Dad asked.

"Mommy!" Blaze cried out.

"Well, that would explain a lot," my Dad said. "Like my Dad always said, one bad apple spoils the whole bunch."

Then we all burst out laughing.

"SHHHHHHH!" my Mom said. "The little baby is sleeping."

Saturday

Wow, what a crazy day I had yesterday.

Well, at least I won't have to worry about getting eaten by a giant Wither.

They decided that the Wither was too dangerous to be kept in the Zoo so they returned it to the Jungle Biome.

Good thing too. I think my uncle was falling in love with it.

Today, Rajit is also heading back to the Endian Biome.

A stretch limo came by the house this morning to pick him up.

As my Mom looked out the window, she called out for Rajit, "Hey Rajit, your ride is here."

As Rajit came down, I started to feel sad that the little guy was going home.

"Thank you, Mr. and Mrs. Zombie, for your great hospitality," Rajit said.

"Anytime Rajit," my Dad said. "It was a pleasure having you in our home."

"More importantly, you saved our son," my Mom said. "And for that we will always be grateful."

It was true. It seems that Rajit wasn't the scared little chicken that I thought.

After I told him that me, Blaze and the guys would hurt him, he went straight to Skelee, Slimey and Creepy, who told Steve, who told my Mom and Dad.

If it wasn't for that little warrior, I would've been Wither chow.

"Rajit, I just wanted to say I was really sorry for being so mean to you the whole time you were here. Sniff… I mean, you've been such a good friend to me this whole time. Sniff… And even after I said I would hurt you if you told on us, you still helped me."

"Zombie, my uncle always told me that friends aren't those that are around when you need them, but rather, they are the ones that need you when you are around," Rajit said.

Whoa.

I didn't really understand what he said, but it sounded really deep.

"Thank you for allowing me to be a friend to you, Zombie," Rajit said. "And I left you a gift in your room to remember me by."

Then Rajit hopped out into his limo and drove away.

As I walked upstairs to my room, I was thinking of Blaze.

It seems that Blaze was so traumatized by the Wither incident that he confessed to burning down his old school. I think they sent him back to the Nether to a school for wayward mobs.

Actually, I think that's the school my uncle Wither teaches at.

When I went into my room, I looked on the dresser where my booger collection normally is.

And I smiled.

Yep. I don't think I will ever forget Rajit for the rest of my life.

Find out What Happens Next in...

Diary of a Minecraft Zombie Book 11
"Insides Out"

Get Your Copy on Amazon Today!

Leave Us a Review

Please support us by leaving a review. The more reviews we get the more books we will write!

And if you really liked this book, please tell a friend. I'm sure they will be happy you told them about it.

Check Out Our Other Books from Zack Zombie Publishing

The Diary of a Minecraft Zombie
Book Series

Get The Entire Series on
Amazon Today!

The Ultimate Minecraft Comic Book Series

Get The Entire Series on Amazon Today!

Herobrine's Wacky
Adventures

Get The Entire Series on
Amazon Today!

The Mobbit

An Unexpected Minecraft Journey

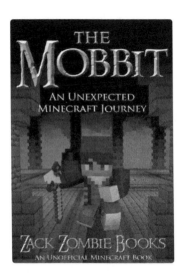

Get The Entire Series on Amazon Today!

Steve Potter and the
Endermen's Stone

Get The Entire Series on
Amazon Today!

An Interview With a
Minecraft Mob

Get The Entire Series on
Amazon Today!

Minecraft
Galaxy Wars

Get The Entire Series on
Amazon Today!

Ultimate Minecraft Secrets:

An Unofficial Guide to Minecraft Tips, Tricks and Hints to Help You Master Minecraft

Get Your Copy on Amazon Today!